FOX AND SQUIRREL

Ruth Ohi

North Winds Press
An Imprint of Scholastic Canada Ltd.

www.scholastic.ca

Library and Archives Canada Cataloguing in Publication
Ohi, Ruth
Fox and Squirrel / by Ruth Ohi.
ISBN 978-1-4431-1914-6
I. Title.
PS8579.H47F69 2013   jC813'.6   C2013-901795-X

Author photo by Annie T.

6 5 4 3 2 1   Printed in Malaysia 108   13 14 15 16 17

For Kaarel — R.O.

"We are very different," said Squirrel.

"Not that different," said Fox.

"You're so big," said Squirrel.

"Not that big," said Fox.

"I like to climb," said Squirrel. "You can't."

"You climb well," said Fox.

Bzzzz

"I live in a nest," said Squirrel.

"You live in a burrow."

"Both are safe and warm," said Fox.

8

"I eat nuts and berries," said Squirrel.

"So do I," said Fox. "Sometimes."

"I like the day," said Squirrel,

"…and you like the night."

"We both like sunsets," said Fox.

"It's raining!" said Squirrel.

"It's raining!" said Fox.

splash!

sploosh!

"How can you two be friends?" said Rat.

"You are both so different!"

16

"Not so different," said Squirrel.

"We both have pointy ears," said Squirrel. "And bushy tails!"

"Well, bushy sometimes," said Fox.

drip

"We both like to run and play…

22

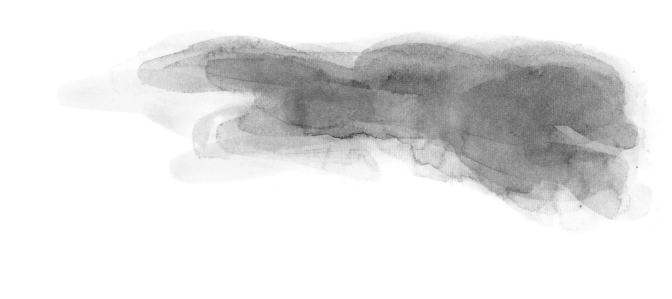

… and rest," said Squirrel.

"*Humph,*" said Rat. "All I can see
are differences."

And then Rat crawled back
into his hole.

"We both get cold," said Squirrel.

Aa-choo

"We both like to be warm," said Fox.

"What are friends for?" said Squirrel.